I CAN BE A SUPERHERO DURING A LOCKDOWN

A SOCIAL STORY BY
RACHEL TEPFER COPELAND

ILLUSTRATED BY
LHAVANYA M.

This book is dedicated to my men.

To my sons—
The world is a better place with both of you in it.
You are exactly the boys I always wanted.

To my husband—
There is no one I would rather share my life with than you.
I love you all more than the world.

I Can Be A Superhero During A Lockdown: A Social Story
Text and illustrations copyright by Mighty Me Publishing
and Rachel Tepfer Copeland, 2018
First edition © 2018. All rights reserved.

Disclaimer: The strategies found within may not be suitable for every situation.
This work is sold with the understanding that neither the author nor the publisher
are held responsible for the results accrued from the strategies in this book.

Authors Acknowledgements: A special thank you to the three wonderful women
who dedicated hours of their time and talent in the creation of this book: My
illustrator Lhavanya M., my editor Lori Blank, and Praise Design Services for
formatting and design.

I want to shout from the rooftops a gigantic thank you to my husband and my
parents. Without each of you, this book would not have been possible. Thank
you so very much for all of your help and support, for believing in my dream and
for making it a reality.

Thank you to Reba, Reid and G for your help and support.

And finally, thank you MR and GS for being my inspiration and my own personal
Superheroes.

ISBN: 978-0-9600653-0-1
Library of Congress Control Number: 2018914340
Written by Rachel Tepfer Copeland
Illustrations by Lhavanya M.
Published by Mighty Me Publishing
RachelTepferCopeland.com

A LETTER TO PARENTS AND EDUCATORS:

We love social stories in our home. Preparing our children is key to empowering and supporting them to become successful in everyday life experiences. Our family uses social stories for a variety of situations- from the mundane everyday life experiences and day to day expectations, to the new and potentially frightening. Social stories are an amazing tool for children of all abilities because these stories are written in a positive, self-affirming, first person account that helps a child visualize a positive ending to a potentially difficult situation.

I Can Be A Superhero During A Lockdown was born out of necessity for my own family. However, once I realized the importance, I decided to publish it to make it available to everyone. One afternoon I went to pick up my son from preschool and he was very obviously shaken and upset. He had a difficult time telling me what had happened. The most I could gather was that the class had played a strange game where the children had hidden in the dark behind backpacks. Hide and seek, I wondered? He shook his head no. Then it dawned on me, it was a Lockdown Drill. The more questions I asked, the more concerned I became. We quickly turned the car around and headed back to speak with the preschool director. After further conversation, we found that my son had become scared, overwhelmed and upset, because he did not know or understand what was happening. He did not feel comfortable hiding with the class in tight quarters. Because of this, he was asked to hide in a different area, away from the rest of the children, to help "decrease his anxiety." I was furious. I was heartbroken. But more than anything, I was scared.

I decided to find a social story that could help him prepare for future Lockdown Drills. However, no matter where I looked, I could only find books for much older children. There was nothing age appropriate or all-encompassing, in a social story format. Additionally, all of the resources I found discussed option based teaching (i.e. run, hide, fight). While these options are incredibly important and frequently successful with adults and teens, many young children and children with special needs become overwhelmed when faced with choices, especially in an active situation. I wanted a book for my son that focused on easy, important skills and, additionally, discussed hiding in depth, as I felt hiding appropriately is very difficult for many young children, including my own. I scoured the internet for a resource fitting these needs, but my search turned up empty. I couldn't stop wonder why, if we prepare our kids for everyday occurrences using social stories, wouldn't we also prepare them for emergency situations? After searching everywhere and finding nothing appropriate, I decided to write my own social story.

I believe that this book will be useful for young children of any ability ages pre k and up, but additionally serve as a valuable tool for children with special needs. It will help them to understand how to handle a Lockdown, what to expect and how to keep themselves safe. My goal was to create a tool for teachers and staff to use to make their days easier and for parents to use for both discussion and preparation at home.

I hope one day this book will be irrelevant and will no longer be needed. Nothing would make me happier than for it to be useless, a thing of the past. It's hard enough sending a young child to school, let alone sending them to school in this scary world. But until that day comes, I hope that this book can help keep our children safe.

Please check out my website RachelTepferCopeland.com for more ways to reinforce the lessons in this book. Also check out Author Rachel Tepfer Copeland on Facebook, Instagram and Pinterest as well for more information. I can be reached by email at RachelTepferCopeland@gmail.com regarding questions, comments, and to request speaking engagements.

Thank you for your purchase. Your support is greatly appreciated. Additionally, I want to thank the true superheroes that keep our kids safe every day, our teachers. You are appreciated more than you know.

Be Safe,
Rachel Copeland

Everywhere we go there are rules. Rules are used to help keep me safe.

When I am at home, some rules that I follow are that I do not touch the oven knobs or answer the door if someone I don't know knocks.

When I ride in the car, a rule that I follow is that I always wear my seatbelt.

When I ride my bike, I wear my helmet. These rules help to keep me safe.

5

My school has rules too. Some rules at school are that I keep my hands and feet to myself and that I raise my hand when I have something to say.

Show & Tell

6

Another school rule is that we practice fire drills. Fire drills are done to make sure that we will be safe if there is a fire at school. I know that when there is a fire drill, I will listen to my teacher and do exactly what she says when the alarm rings. This is an important rule that keeps me safe.

CLASS 152

Another drill my school has is a Lockdown Drill. Drills help to keep me safe. Everyone has jobs to do during a drill. I have jobs too! If I can do my jobs during a drill, then I will keep myself, my friends, and my teacher safe.

A Lockdown Drill is a drill that is used to practice how to keep myself, my friends, and my teacher safe if someone who is not allowed to come into our school comes inside. A Lockdown can also be used for other reasons, such as when adults believe it is best that we stay safe indoors. Just like a fire drill, we won't know if a Lockdown is a practice drill, or really happening, until after it is over. I will always do my jobs just in case it is a real Lockdown and not a drill.

EXIT

To keep myself, my friends and my teacher safe, I have some very important jobs. They are not easy. I will have to work very hard. Can I do it?

These are my jobs during a Lockdown. When I do these jobs, I will help to keep myself, my friends, and my teacher safe!

My jobs are:

1. I will listen to my teacher, or the adult in charge, and follow all of their directions.

2. I will stay very, very quiet.

3. I will stay very, very still in my hiding spot until my teacher, or the adult in charge, tells me it is ok to move.

When I do my jobs, I keep myself and everyone else safe. When I do my jobs, I am a Superhero!

There are all kinds of superheroes. Some superheroes stop bad guys. Some superheroes keep people safe by helping people or doing other very important jobs. I will be a Superhero who helps other people. I will be a Superhero by helping to keep myself, my friends, and my teacher safe by doing my very important jobs. I will help others by using my super abilities to listen closely to my teacher, or the adult in charge, stay as quiet as a silent mouse, and as still as a statue.

It is very important that I let the police stop the bad guys because I will be busy doing my important jobs. The police keep me safe and, when I do my jobs, I will help to keep everyone else safe! When we work together as a team, we can all be safe!

EXIT

When I follow the directions of my teacher, or the adult in charge, keep quiet, and stay still in my hiding spot, I make sure that we can all hide safely until the Lockdown is over. When I do my jobs, I help others by keeping myself and everyone else safe. When I do my jobs, I am a Superhero.

I know that these jobs will not be easy for me and I will have to work very hard. That is why doing these jobs makes me a Superhero. Superheroes don't have easy jobs, but I know that I can do it.

When a Lockdown happens, someone may come over the announcements to tell us that it is a Lockdown or my teacher may tell our class. It may be while I am in the middle of working or playing.

It may be when I am busy. I might be eating lunch in the cafeteria, going to the bathroom, or playing at recess. I may not want to stop what I am doing.

But I will follow the rules, so I can stay safe and help to keep my friends and teacher safe. I will do my jobs. I can be a Superhero by doing my jobs and working to keep myself, and everyone else, safe.

17

My teacher, or the adult in charge, will turn off the lights. It will be very dark. I will be very, very quiet. I will follow the directions of my teacher, or the adult in charge. I will quickly hide wherever I am told to hide. I will stay in that spot and will be very still and very quiet, even if I don't want to. If my teacher tells me to run, I will run. I will always do exactly what my teacher, or the adult in charge, tells me to do right away.

My teacher, or the adult in charge, will tell me where to hide. Some of my friends may be told to hide behind our desks, or in a closet, or in the bathroom. We might have to hide in the library or in the cafeteria. I may not want to hide where my teacher, or the adult in charge, tells me to hide, but I will quickly and quietly hide wherever I am told to hide, even if I don't want to. I will follow directions and do what I am told to do quickly and quietly. This is part of doing my job and being a Superhero.

Sometimes I will have to hide next to a lot of people. It can be hard work hiding next to a lot of people in the dark. I will remember that it is very important for me to be very, very still and very, very quiet. I will stay still and quiet. I will keep myself and my friends safe. I will do my Superhero jobs.

I might have to hide in a bathroom. If I am alone in the bathroom when there is a Lockdown, I will stay in the bathroom and hide until I am told it is over on the announcements. I might have to sit on the bathroom floor or sit or stand on a toilet. I do not have to worry about germs during a Lockdown. I can change into new clothes to wear after the Lockdown is over if I am worried about germs. I can cover my nose if it smells bad and I can shut my eyes. But I will do my jobs. I will work to keep myself, my friends, and my teacher safe by doing my important jobs. Then I will be a Superhero.

A Lockdown might happen while I am in the cafeteria, the gym, or the library. It might happen while I am playing outside, going to the bathroom or getting a drink from the water fountain. I might have to hide in an area that is not my regular classroom or even a place I have never been to before.

I might have a teacher that I don't know tell me where to go and where to hide. No matter where I am or who is helping me, I will listen to the adult in charge and follow their directions. If I am alone, or there is no adult nearby, then I will find a safe place to hide and I will stay there quietly until I am told the Lockdown is over. It is important that I do my jobs.

When I hide, I will work very hard to do my jobs to stay very, very still and very, very quiet. I can shut my eyes when I am hiding and think of things that make me feel happy. I can think of my favorite TV show or movie, my pet or my family, or I can imagine myself in a place that makes me feel happy and safe. What are some things I might think of?

24

Sometimes Lockdowns take a short time and sometimes Lockdowns take a long time. I will use my patience. I will do my important jobs. When the Lockdown takes a long time, I might get tired of hiding or I might think of something I want to say. I might want to turn on the light and move around. It might be hard to stay still and stay quiet. It might be boring. I might feel a little bit scared. However, I know that if I talk or move or turn on the light before the Lockdown is over, I will not be safe. I will keep myself safe. I will do my important jobs. I will do all my jobs even if I don't want to.

I follow rules to help keep myself, my friends, and my teacher safe. When I follow rules, I am a Superhero. I listen to my teacher, or other adults in charge, and follow their directions. I will run if the adult in charge tells me to run. I will hide if the adult in charge tells me to hide. I know to stay very still and very quiet when I hide during Lockdowns. I am good at my jobs.

I will know that the Lockdown is over when I am told that it is over on the announcements, or the adult in charge tells me that it is over. When the Lockdown is over, I will know that we are safe. When the Lockdown is over, my teacher will turn on the lights. We will stop hiding and we will go back to doing our work.

Can I do my jobs? Can I help to keep myself, my friends, and my teacher safe? Can I be a Superhero? It won't be easy. It will be hard work. Can I do it?

Yes I can!

What are the important
jobs that I will do to
be a Superhero during
a Lockdown?

Say them loud
and proud!

1. I will listen to my teacher, or the adult in charge, and follow all of their directions.

2. I will stay very, very quiet.

3. I will stay very, very still in my hiding spot until my teacher, or the adult in charge, tells me it is ok to move.

I will do my jobs. I will be a Superhero.

I CAN BE A SUPERHERO DURING A LOCKDOWN

Made in the USA
Middletown, DE
07 October 2020